For: Iggy, JoAnn,
Tyler, John, Gabrielle, Giana, & Dominic

Remember—

Never Turn A lovely Soul Away!

The Story Master

2008

The Keeper at the Inn

Written by
Steve McCurdy

Illustrated by
Stephanie Lohmann

The Keeper at the Inn

Written by Steve McCurdy

Cover Design and Illustrations by Stephanie Lohmann

Published by: StoryMaster Press, 14520 Memorial Drive, Suite M-141, Houston, Texas 77077, 281-920-0442

info@storymasterpress.com , www.storymasterpress.com

Printed in the USA

ISBN: 978-0-9761179-2-6

10 9 8 7 6 5 4 3 2 1

   If you are unable to purchase this book from your bookseller, you may order directly from the publisher's website.

   The Audio CD of this story is attached on the inside back cover. It contains an introduction and one track of audio for each two page spread in the book. You may let the CD play or you can use your CD player's NEXT TRACK button to skip to the next set of pages at any time.

My name is Jaiphus. I'm a very old man.
And I've a story I think you should hear.
Of an evening-like this-a very long time ago.
Even before I was born, my dear.

Yes, it began a long, long time ago,
Beneath a rock, near the bottom of a hill.
A young man and woman started this story,
And the best part of it continues still.

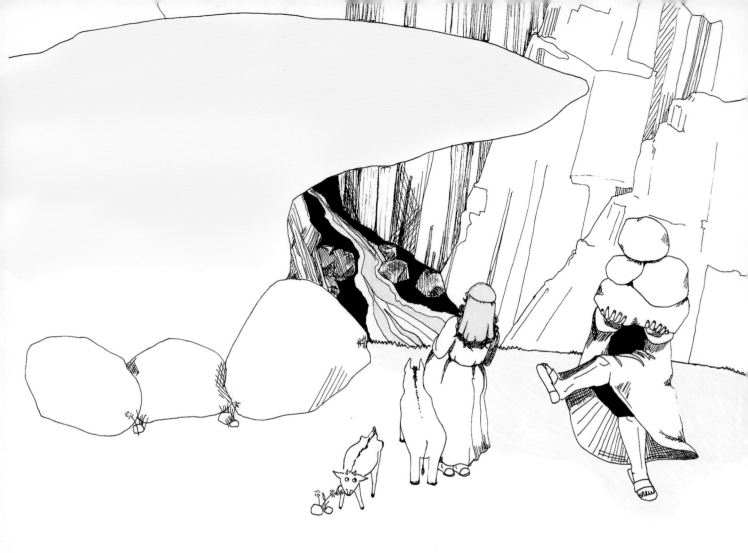

Finding no neighborhoods in that region,
   With nice houses ready to move into,
   The young woman said,
        "Let's live in the shelter of this stone."

        And the young man started building a lean-to.

As the years went by, he added strong walls,
to keep the wind and the weather out.

And they decided their family could prosper there.
Oh, of that, they had very little doubt.

Well, I was born inside that tiny space.
And my father, quick, smart, and able...
Made a cradle for me
from the cow's feeding trough.

You see, our house was also...
our stable.

All my brothers were born
  and cradled there as well.
    I thought we'd live there all of our lives...
      'till we died.

That all changed when my sister,
  Eliana, came along.
    Because THIS is how she cried....

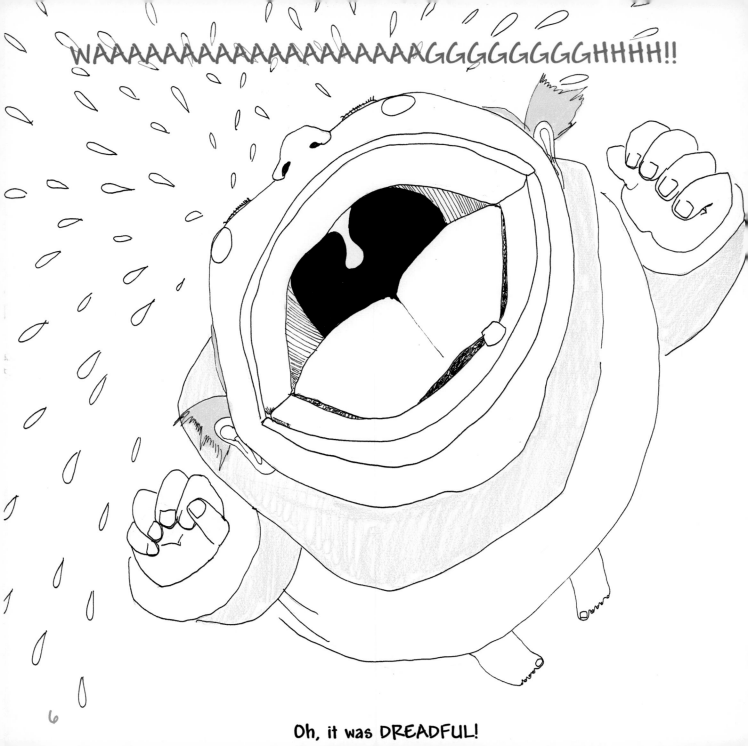

Oh, it was DREADFUL!

Now, as crowded as it was in that little room,
It was even more so with the animals in.
So, Eliana gets the credit
for our new living space.

The building of the house
began to begin.

My father was a wonderful builder-man whiz
with tools, and with stone and with wood.
When it came to mechanicals, everyone agreed.
My father was great. Not just good!

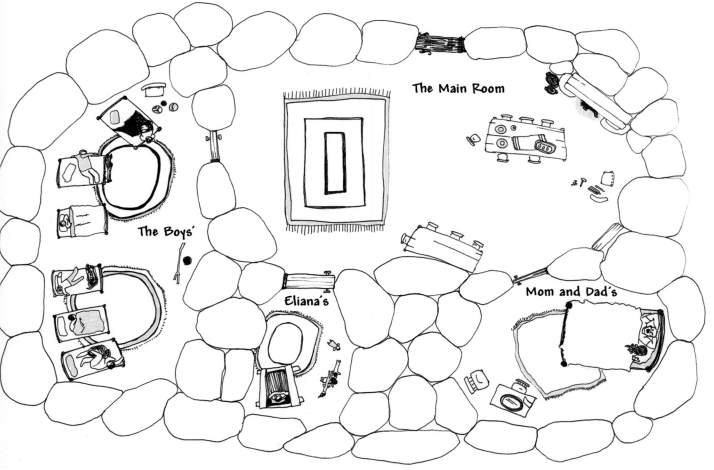

The Main Room

The Boys'

Eliana's

Mom and Dad's

He built a house with four rooms,
One for him and our mother,
One for all of us boys,
With Eliana's FAR from any other!

The room we cooked, ate and lived in,
Was wonderful, open and large.

Room for Father to build his furniture
And for Mother to firmly take charge.

9

The strong, thick walls he built,
withstood every season's test.

But Eliana's walls were the thickest.
Thicker by far than all the rest.

"It's a fortress for our little princess,"
Mom and Dad would say with pride.
But if the truth be known -
    It was so they could be alone!
    They couldn't hear her -
    When she was inside!

10

Father, then began building furniture,
    for all the folks around our town.

Mother took to making their clothing.
    Seems we always had people around.

Our main room was built out larger.
    Rooms got added, here and there.

Visitors passing through would ask to stay.
    We'd have folks sleeping EVERYwhere.

MORE BEDS
UPSTAIRS

11

Once a man admired our wide front door.
Father showed him how he'd carefully cut it in.

"You're a great builder of houses," said the man.

"Houses?" said another –

"I thought this was an inn."

Father had never stopped to think about it,
He'd just done the things he knew how to do.
"These folks say we're an Inn," he said to Mom.
"I suppose so, dear. Hurry up. Lots to do."

"Put more water in the soup, Eliana,"
Mother would shout from the greeting door.

"We'll need more meat, more meal, more bread."
Father's say, "Yes. There's always room for more."

I think people were friendlier then, than now.
I just remember how my father would say...

"Yes, I know it's inconvenient... You sleep right over here."

"Son, try to never turn a lonely soul away."

My brothers grew up
and they married.

Eliana, too...
They all moved away.

But, since we didn't have their
gifts and talents,
My wife and I decided we'd stay.

We took care of my parents
as they grew old.

When guests were in
we cared for them
as well.

And on nights when it
was just the four of us home....

Then, old innkeeper stories we'd tell.

15

When my parents passed on,
I wasn't sure what to do.
But, my wife stood in the big
hearty kitchen...

And with hands on her hips,
said, "Jiaphus, get busy!

YOU'RE the innkeeper now.

It's tradition."

As the years went by,
we fared well enough.

Though newer inns had emerged,
here and there.

My wife's wonderful cooking
wore out THREE cooking pots.

While all I wore out...
was my hair.

17

Then a decree went out
from Caesar Augustus,
Seems all the world was
to be TAXED!

DECREE of

TAXATION

Everyman must return to his home,
to be counted.

That meant GUESTS! Quick!
All the chairs must be waxed!!

In anticipation of my imminent wealth,
I made all the rooms
ready as could be.

Then all my brothers arrived,
with their children, and wives.

All expecting rooms -
HERE...

And for free!

Eliana and her lout of a husband, too!!

I had two paying guests,
     and twenty-nine relatives,
          All wanting rooms - with a VIEW!

     "Why should we PAY
          to stay in our own HOME???"

They were right.

                    There was nothing I could do.

All day long I turned them away.
Lonely, dusty travelers,
desperately EAGER to PAY!!!

If my family would have SHARED,
I could have still made a go...

But SHARE? Share my SPACE? Are you MAD?

Heavens NO!!

At sunset he came and knocked on my door.
"Go away, I'm full up. I can't take anymore!"

"That's too bad," he said, as his hand rubbed the frame.
"All the inns are full.
Everywhere the story's the same.
But this workmanship is fine.
I wish we could have stayed."

Then he turned to press on.
The sun would not
be delayed.

Then I saw his tired
little donkey.
And on it, his
tired little wife.

I had never wished I was an only child
So much in my entire life.

And then... I had an idea!

"Young man," I said,
"I do have a spot...
Now, I warn you,
It's not fancy or fine.

"But if you'd care to have a look,
I can take you 'round back."

And he said,

"Let's see what you have in mind."

Now, I was born and raised in that stable.
All my family had lived there as well.

But the look on his face
Spoke loud and clear...
This was not what he wanted,
I could tell.

"I have nothing better to offer you son.
You are welcome to this, if you dare.

Perhaps your young wife could rest here
for a bit, while you search for
something better-elsewhere?"

24

And I believe that is precisely what he would have done,
But it was her words that then changed his mind...

"Let it be, Joseph.
This will serve our needs.

Thank you, Innkeeper,
You have been
very kind."

I fell in love with that child,
right there, on the spot.

There was little for her
I would not have done.

I spread fresh straw,
To make things look nice.

25

But, in moving the manger,

It came all undone.

"Mary, I can repair this, if he has a few tools."
Said the young woman's strong, tender man.

She looked to me, I opened a door...
My father's tools I placed in the carpenter's hand.

With him busy at work, and she settling in,
I began to feel better. And right.

They were as comfortable
as this Keeper of the Inn
Could make anyone,
on this Bethlehem night.

Duties in the house called me to task.
We fed them all and got them to bed.

28

But the peace wouldn't last.
A pounding came on my door.

And the voice life had taught me
most to dread.

29

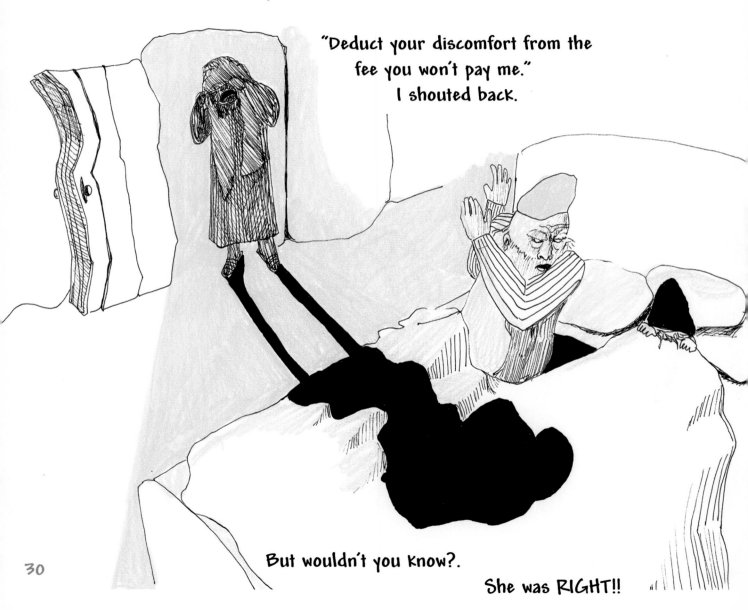

"Jiaphus!" she cried as she pounded.
"We can't sleep with this light
that's so BRIGHT!"

"Deduct your discomfort from the
fee you won't pay me."
I shouted back.

30

But wouldn't you know?.

She was RIGHT!!

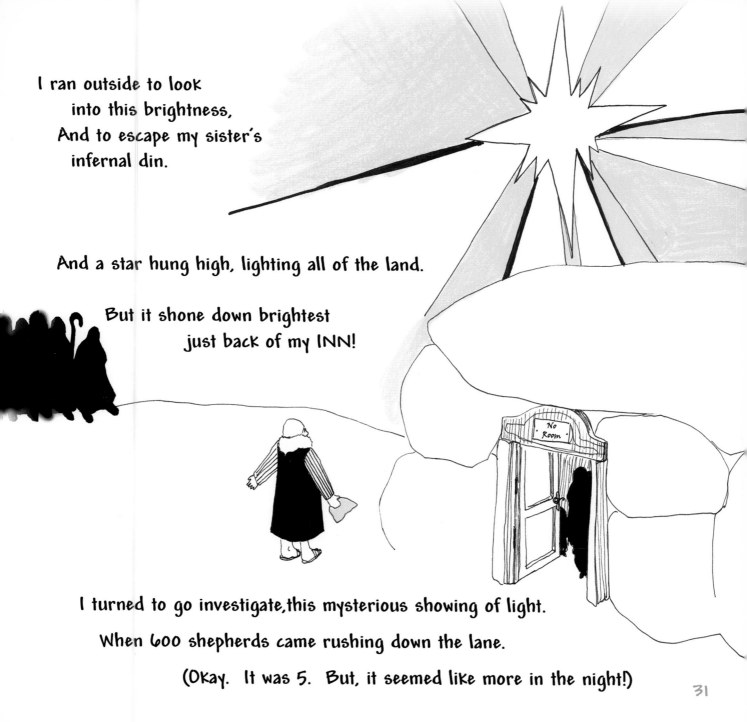

I ran outside to look
   into this brightness,
And to escape my sister's
   infernal din.

And a star hung high, lighting all of the land.

   But it shone down brightest
         just back of my INN!

No
Room

I turned to go investigate, this mysterious showing of light.

When 600 shepherds came rushing down the lane.

   (Okay. It was 5. But, it seemed like more in the night!)

31

One of them grabbed me up by my lapels.
Another yelled...
   "Where's the child that we seek???"

"CHILDREN?" says I....
   "I have an Inn-full right here.
      They're yours for the asking,
         sweet and meek."

Then, they told me the story
of the angel's words.

Singing praises and
heralding on high...

Of the Christ Child,
    born in a stable that night.

I knew of a stable -
    a stable VERY near by.

33

They rounded the house much
    faster than I.

I had to push my way through
    begging, "Please."

But when I arrived, I was in for
    the shock of my life.

All the shepherds were there.
    on their knees.

34

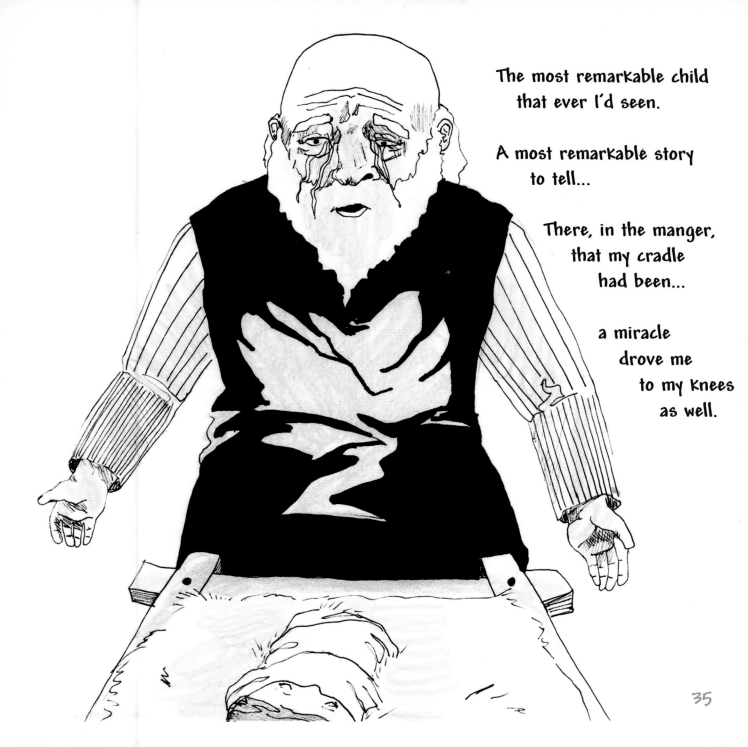

The most remarkable child
that ever I'd seen.

A most remarkable story
to tell...

There, in the manger,
that my cradle
had been...

a miracle
drove me
to my knees
as well.

35

For, I don't know how it is
that I knew... what I knew.
... But I knew.

He was the King - you see?

The King had come into the world,
into my very world.

and he'd come - just exactly - like me.

Dedication

For the children who inspired it - Chase, Chelsea, Ashlee - and now, Connor. And for the woman who insisted it be put to page - Ruth.